Ethel the Emu

written by
Pamela Wiley

illustrated by
Robin DeWitt and
Patricia DeWitt Grush

KAEDEN BOOKS

Title: Ethel the Emu
Copyright © 2007 Kaeden Corporation
Author: Pamela Wiley
Illustrators: Robin DeWitt and Patricia DeWitt Grush

ISBN: 978-1-57874-335-3

Published by:
      Kaeden Corporation
      P.O. Box 16190
      Rocky River, Ohio 44116
      1-800-890-7323
      www.kaeden.com

Printed in Canada

10 9 8 7 6 5 4 3 2 1

Contents

—1—

A Farm for Sale

Mom was reading from the newspaper. "The listing says E M U does not convey."

"What's 'listing'?" asked Sadie.

"It's a description of a property that someone is trying to sell," answered Mom. "The whole listing says: '11 acres, 2 barns, 4 small sheds, large greenhouse, brick farmhouse, 3 bedrooms, 2 baths, screened-in porch, small tractor with implements, E M U does not convey.' "

"What does 'convey' mean?" asked Jonah.

" 'Convey' means it goes along with the property automatically. Whatever E M U is, it doesn't stay with the farm when someone buys it," said Mom. "I wonder what E M U stands for. Hmm. Electro-Magnetic Unit? Energy Management Utility? Maybe it has something to do with the greenhouse."

"Every Mole Underground!" said Jonah.

"Early Morning Underpants!" contributed Grace.

"Eggs Make U strong!" offered Sadie.

"Stop! Stop!" cried Mom with a chuckle. "I'll ask tomorrow."

—2—

E M U

"Guess what?" said Mom the next day. "It's not E M U. It's emu!"

"What's 'emu'?" asked Sadie.

"It's a great big bird that comes from Australia," said Grace.

"Right," said Mom. "The emu has very long legs, a long bluish-black neck, and a small head with a sharp beak."

"Does it fly?" asked Jonah.

"I don't think so," said Mom.

EMU

Dromaius novaehollandiae)

Height: 2m (6ft. 6in.)

Feathers of the Emu are unusual

Feathers grow out of one quill

IND E

Emu egg

"Does it convey?" asked Sadie.

"No, honey. Mr. Reynolds wants to keep the emu with him when he moves," said Mom. "She's his pet. Her name is Ethel."

"Too bad," said Sadie. "I like emus."

"How do you know?" asked Grace.

"I just do," said Sadie. "Eee-moo. Eee-moo."

"Can we buy the farm anyway?" asked Jonah.

"Let's go look at it," said Mom.

—3—

Meeting Ethel

"There she is!" cried Sadie. "Eee-moo. Eee-moo."

"She looks like an ostrich," said Grace.

"She looks like a great big turkey on stilts," said Jonah.

"She's just tall," said Sadie. "Hi, Ethel."

"What's that sound?" asked Mom.

"It sounds like a bongo drum or a tom-tom," said Grace.

"It's coming from Ethel's throat," said Jonah.

"Cool!" said Grace.

"That must be her way of talking to us. I think she's saying 'Hi'," said Mom.

"Eee-moo. Pah-bum! Eee-moo. Pah-bum, pah-bum, pah-bum!" said Sadie.

Mom, Jonah, Grace, and Sadie looked around the farm and went into all the buildings. Jonah and Grace climbed up on the tractor and pretended to drive it. Then they all went into the house.

"I like the fireplaces," said Grace.

"I like the porch swing," said Jonah.

"I like the eee-moo," said Sadie. "Eee-moo. Eee-moo. Pah-bum, pah-bum, pah-bum! Pah-bum, pah-bum, pah-bum!"

Then Mom said, "Mr. Reynolds, we like your farm very much and we would like to buy it and live here."

"Great!" said Mr. Reynolds. "I think you'll like living here. There is a lot to do. I'll come to take Ethel as soon as you move in."

"Does that mean Ethel doesn't convey?" asked Sadie.

"I'm afraid it does," said Mom. "She'll be moving with Mr. Reynolds."

—4—

Moving In

On moving day, Mr. Reynolds stopped by and said, "I see you have almost everything moved in. Welcome to the farm. I'll come back tomorrow with my truck to pick up Ethel. See you tomorrow."

"I want Ethel to convey," said Sadie. "I like her."

"I like that drumming sound she makes," said Grace. "It's so relaxing."

"I like Ethel too," said Mom, "but she belongs to Mr. Reynolds. Besides, she's not very useful. We'll get some chickens to put in that pen instead. They're useful. We can always use chicken eggs."

"How do you think Mr. Reynolds will catch Ethel?" asked Jonah. "She is so big."

"I guess we'll see tomorrow," said Mom.

—5—

Moving Ethel

The next day Mr. Reynolds arrived in his truck. He parked it next to Ethel's pen. He took a big sack out of the truck, opened the gate and walked in. When he went toward Ethel with the sack, she started running around frantically. Her neck jerked back and forth and her eyes darted around looking for an escape. She tried to jump over the fence but it was too high and she fell back into the pen.

"I guess emus can't fly," said Grace.

Mr. Reynolds chased Ethel around the pen for a long time.

"I don't think he can catch her," said Jonah.

"Maybe he is trying to tire her out," said Grace.

In a little while, Ethel did get tired and Mr. Reynolds got close enough to throw the sack over her head.

"Emus are like ostriches," Mr. Reynolds said. "They feel safe with their heads in the ground."

"Or in a sack," said Sadie.

"Right!" said Mr. Reynolds. "I guess darkness makes them feel safe."

Mr. Reynolds started pushing Ethel toward the truck. He almost had her inside when Ethel suddenly shook her head back and forth. The sack flew off her head. Ethel jumped through the space between the truck and the pen

and ran out into the field. Mr. Reynolds ran after her. His dog jumped through the window of the truck and chased after both of them.

"Oh, no!" yelled Mom. "That's a bulldog. If he catches Ethel, he will grab her by the throat and not let go."

"Her throat is pretty big," said Grace.

"Look at Ethel run!" said Jonah.

"Go Ethel!" said Sadie.

Ethel lowered her head and stretched out her long neck and

long legs. She easily kept ahead of Mr. Reynolds and his dog. They ran back and forth in the big field for a long time.

"She doesn't even look like she is running," said Grace. "She's gliding!"

"I think Ethel is going to tire them out," said Jonah.

"I think you're right," said Mom. "Her legs are so long that each stride covers a lot of ground. She's keeping far ahead of them and that dog is fast!"

Soon the dog came back to the house panting and flopped down on the grass. Mr. Reynolds also gave up and walked back to the truck.

"Now what will we do?" asked Mom.

Mr. Reynolds said, "Don't worry. Just leave Ethel's gate open and some food in her pan. She'll come back when she is hungry."

—6—

Moving Ethel Again

Three days later Ethel had found her way back into her pen and was eating hungrily. Mom called Mr. Reynolds and he came back in his truck. This time he had the sack and a long rope. He made a loop on the end of the rope and went into the pen. Ethel started running around in circles again.

"Emus can't walk or run backwards. They can only go forward," said Jonah.

"How do you know that?" asked Mom.

"I looked it up. Australians use them as an unofficial symbol of their country because they are always moving forward," said Jonah.

"I know something about emus too," said Grace. "The mommy emus don't sit on the eggs. The daddy emus hatch the eggs. They can sit on the eggs for eight weeks without eating or drinking. I looked it up."

"Wow!" said Mom. "That is very interesting."

Mr. Reynolds chased Ethel until they were both tired and then he

threw the rope around her neck. He pulled the rope down around her chest and put the sack over her head. Then he tried to pull her toward the truck. Ethel wouldn't budge.

"I know something about emus too," said Sadie. "They are strong! I didn't have to look it up!"

Jonah and Grace joined Mom and Mr. Reynolds and they all pulled and pulled. Ethel started to move a little. Then, all of a sudden, she laid down on the ground gasping. Loud croaking sounds came from her throat.

"Is she choking?" asked Grace.

Ethel made a few more gasping noises and then laid her head down. She stopped moving.

"Oh, dear," said Mr. Reynolds. "I hope we didn't hurt her."

He knelt down beside Ethel and laid his head against her side. "She's still breathing and her heart is pumping," said Mr. Reynolds. "Let's pick her up and carry her to the truck."

Ethel was very heavy but Mom and Mr. Reynolds carefully picked her up and slowly carried her toward the truck. When they almost had her in the truck, Ethel suddenly lifted her head and threw off the sack again. Then she jumped out of their arms, gave one last tug and snapped the rope!

"There she goes again," said Sadie.

"There she goes again all right,"
said Mr. Reynolds. "There's no use
chasing her. I'll have to go home
without her. Call me when she
comes back."

—7—

A Job for Ethel

When Ethel was back, Mr. Reynolds came again and said, "I don't think Ethel wants to move with me. I think she wants to stay here with your family."

"Is Ethel going to convey?" asked Sadie, jumping up and down and clapping her hands.

"Oh, please Mommy, can we keep her?" asked Grace.

"Well, I don't know," said Mom. "She's not very useful. We already

have a lot to take care of. We were going to put chickens in that pen. We can use the eggs."

"I can build another pen for the chickens," said Jonah.

"I'll help you," said Mr. Reynolds. "We should build it right next to Ethel's pen. The foxes are a real problem around here. They are very clever and can get into most any chicken coop. Fortunately, foxes are afraid of big birds like emus so they won't disturb the chickens if Ethel is nearby."

"So Ethel would be useful!" said Grace. "She would be the chicken coop guard!"

"That's true!" said Mr. Reynolds.

"Well, imagine that!" said Mom.

Jonah and Mr. Reynolds found some

old boards and a roll of chicken wire in the barn. They built a chicken coop next to Ethel's pen. Everybody helped. Mom bought a dozen chickens from the man at the Feed Store. Mr. Reynolds picked them up in his truck and put them in the new chicken coop next to Ethel. Grace fed the chickens every day. After a few weeks,

she started finding eggs every morning in the nesting boxes.

"Yum, yum," said Mom. "There's nothing like fresh eggs! They make everything taste better."

Sadie counted the chickens every day and came in the house with her report: "Twelve chickens. Zero foxes."

"Ethel is doing her job!" said Mom. "I guess we'll have to keep her."

"Hurray!" said Grace. "Ethel stays!"

"Hurray!" said Jonah. "Persistence pays!"

"Hurray!" said Sadie. "Happy days!"

"Hurray!" cried everyone. "Ethel conveys!"